What Is Budu?

Written by **Billie Huban**

CARAMEL TREE

Budu lives in the jungle.
He lives with the animals.

"What am I?" says Budu.

"I am a wolf!"
"No, no, no," says the wolf.
"You do not have long fur."

"I am a monkey!"
"No, no, no," says the monkey.
"You do not have a long tail."

"I am a giraffe!"
"No, no, no," says the giraffe.
"You do not have a long neck."

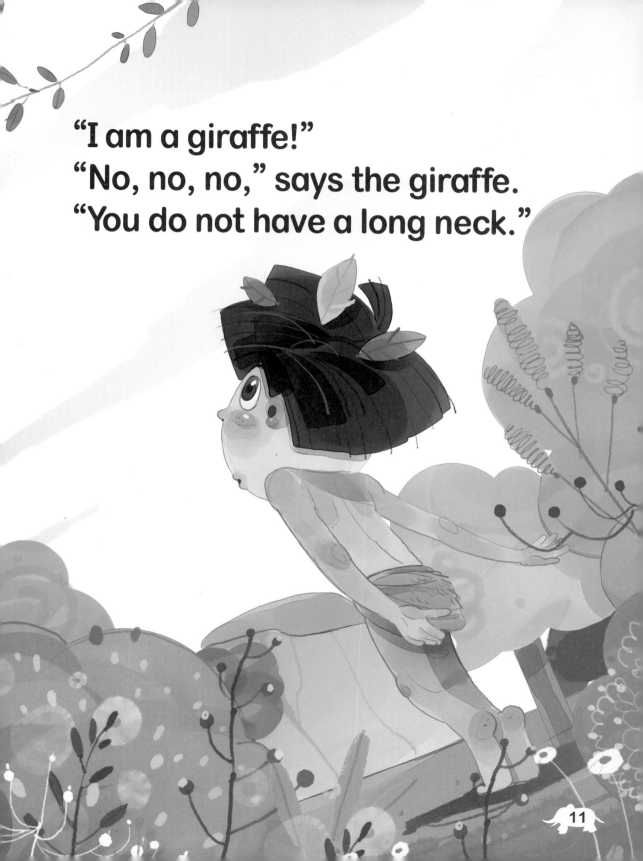

Chapter 2 Not Big?

"I am an elephant!"
"No, no, no," says the elephant.
"You do not have big ears."

13

"I am an owl!"
"No, no, no," says the owl.
"You do not have big eyes."

"I am a hippo!"
"No, no, no," says the hippo.
"You do not have a big mouth."

"I am a lion!"
"No, no, no," says the lion.
"You do not have big teeth."

"I am an ant!"
"No, no, no," says the ant.
"You are too big!"

Chapter 3

What Is Budu?

"What am I?"
Budu looks in the lake.

"I have a face with two eyes and two ears."

"I have a nose and a mouth."

"I have two arms and two hands."

"I have two legs and two feet."

"What am I?" says Budu.

"I am a boy!" Budu smiles.